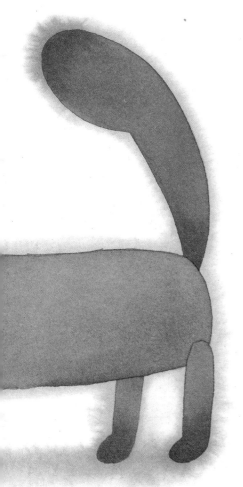

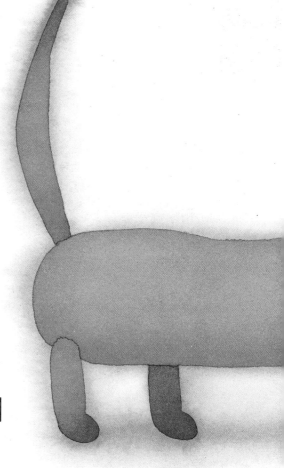

Un gato y un perro

A Cat and a Dog

escrito por Claire Masurel
ilustrado por Bob Kolar

traducido por Andrés Antreasyan

SCHOLASTIC INC.

New York   Toronto   London   Auckland
Sydney   New Delhi   Hong Kong

For Mathilde —C.M.
For Olivia —B.K.

Text copyright © 2001 by Claire Masurel.
Illustrations copyright © 2001 by Bob Kolar.
Spanish translation copyright © 2003 by North-South Books Inc.
All rights reserved. Published by Scholastic Inc., 557 Broadway, New York, NY 10012,
by arrangement with North-South Books Inc.
Printed in the U.S.A.

ISBN-13: 978-0-545-27014-4
ISBN-10: 0-545-27014-6

17 18 19 20   40   19 18 17

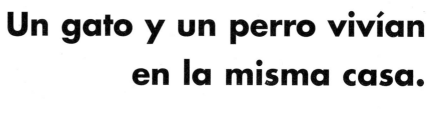

Un gato y un perro vivían en la misma casa.

A cat and a dog lived in the same house.

Pero *no* eran amigos.
But they were *not* friends.

HSSS!

HSSS!

GRRR!

GRRR!

Peleaban todo el tiempo,

They fought all the time,

¡Perro torpe!

Clumsy dog!

noche . . .

night . . .

¡Gato molesto!

Fussy cat!

y día.
and day.

¡Perro sucio!
Dirty dog!

¡Gato perezoso!
Lazy cat!

Peleaban por todo,

They fought about everything,

los mejores lugares,

the best spots,

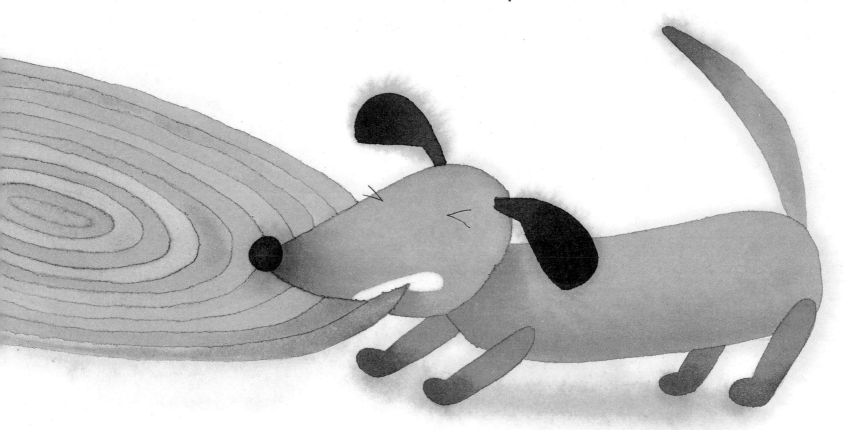

la mejor comida.

the best treats.

Pero más que nada, peleaban por los juguetes.

But most of all, they fought about their toys.

HSSS!

HSSS!

¿Ves estas garras? ¡No te acerques a mi ratoncito!

See these claws? Stay away from my mouse!

GRRR!

GRRR!

¿Ves estos colmillos? ¡No te acerques a mi pelota!
See these fangs? Stay away from my ball!

El gato y el perro jugaban solos.

The cat and the dog played on their own.

Mordisqueando

Chewing

Persiguiendo

Chasing

Rodando

Rolling

Atrapando

Catching

Hasta que un día, pasó algo terrible.

Then one day, something terrible happened.

¡OH, NO!

OH, NO!

No sé nadar.

I can't swim.

¡OH, NO!
OH, NO!

No sé trepar.

I can't climb.

No había absolutamente nada que pudieran hacer.

There was absolutely nothing they could do.

¿Nada?
Nothing?

¡Ya sé!
I know!

¡Yo sé nadar!

I can swim!

¡Yo sé trepar!
I can climb!

¡Toma, Gato!
Here, Cat!

¡Toma, Perro!

Here, Dog!

**Un gato y un perro viven
en la misma casa . . .**

A cat and a dog live
in the same house . . .

y ahora son los mejores amigos.
and now they are the best of friends.